WILLIAM H. HOOKS

Freedom's Fruit

PAINTINGS BY
JAMES RANSOME

ALFRED A. KNOPF ❧ NEW YORK

For Priscilla Pemberton and Lonetta Gaines

—W. H. H.

To Mother Margaret...thanks for all your love and support

—J. R.

THIS IS A BORZOI BOOK PUBLISHED BY ALFRED A. KNOPF, INC.

Text copyright © 1996 by William H. Hooks
Illustrations copyright © 1996 by James Ransome
All rights reserved under International and Pan-American Copyright Conventions.
Published in the United States of America by Alfred A. Knopf, Inc., New York, and
simultaneously in Canada by Random House of Canada Limited, Toronto.
Distributed by Random House, Inc., New York.

Library of Congress Cataloging-in-Publication Data
Hooks, William H.
Freedom's fruit / by William H. Hooks ; illustrated by James Ransome.
p.   cm.
Summary: Mama Marina, a slave woman and conjurer in the Old South, casts a
spell on her master's grapes as part of her plan to win freedom for her daughter
Sheba and the man Sheba loves.
ISBN 0-679-82438-3 (trade) — ISBN 0-679-92438-8 (lib. bdg.)
[1. Slavery—Fiction. 2. Afro-Americans—Fiction. 3. Magic—Fiction.]
I. Ransome, James, ill   II. Title.
PZ7.H7664Fr   1995
[Fic]—dc20   93-235

Manufactured in Singapore
2 4 6 8 0 9 7 5 3

AUTHOR'S NOTE

In the "Low Country," along the coasts of the Carolinas, the practice of conjuring has existed for over three hundred years. It was a deeply ingrained part of the life of the Africans who were brought as slaves to this part of the New World.

A conjure man or woman could cast spells and remove spells, or offer protection from the dire consequences of spells. Spell casting was usually accompanied by the use of roots, herbs, and parts of small animals such as chicken hearts or toad livers. Often a bit of hair, a toenail clipping, or a drop of blood was required from the one being conjured. But the essential ingredient in the conjuring process was the complete conviction on the part of all concerned that the spell would work.

Growing up in the Carolina Low Country, I heard many tales about conjurers and spell casting, and they seemed much more real to me than the evil witches and fairy godmothers in my storybooks. Conjurers were right in our neighborhood. Dr. Buzzard, the most famous conjure man in Columbus County, lived only a half-hour away.

Freedom's Fruit is based on a conjure tale I heard in my childhood. Later, when I read the Greek myths, I was struck by the tale's similarity to the Persephone story, in which a human life follows the birth, flourishing, dying, and rebirth cycle of the annual growing season.

Today there are only a few conjure people left. What remains is a rich body of tales that linger in the oral tradition and reveal to us the magic and power of these people.

Mama Marina was a slave woman, but she was no ordinary slave. She was a conjure woman who could cast powerful spells, as well as protect people from evil spirits.

One day Mama Marina was surprised to see Master Alston standing in her cabin door.

"Morning, sir," she said.

"Anybody around?" asked Master Alston.

"No, sir," she answered.

"Where's that daughter of yours?"

"Off rambling in the woods for huckleberries. You need Sheba, sir?"

"Just wanted to make sure we're alone," answered the master. "I've a piece of work for you to do."

"Yes, sir."

"Now, you know I don't set store by this conjure business. But I'm put out, Marina. I've threatened and I've even laid on the whip, but it does no good. My fine wine grapes get eaten up each year by my slaves as soon as they ripen."

The master turned away, mumbling a curse under his breath.

"You say you got a piece of work for me, sir?" asked Mama Marina.

"Yes, by God, I do. I want you to conjure the grapes. But nobody's to know it's on orders from me."

The master started to leave.

"One thing, sir," called Mama Marina. "I need one thing from you to make it work."

"What's that?" asked the master.

"A piece of gold," she whispered.

The master dug into his pocket and handed Mama Marina a small gold piece.

"How many of these I need to buy my daughter's freedom?" she asked.

The master laughed. "You'd need a hundred to buy Sheba's freedom, a fine strong slave like her."

"Thank you, sir," said Mama Marina. "Tonight the word will go out. Them grapes be conjured. Much as everybody craves sweet grapes in season, nobody dare lay a hand on conjured grapes."

The master left Mama Marina's cabin. She closed the door and hid the small gold piece in a money belt she wore under her clothes. Through the years as a conjure woman, she had managed to collect gold pieces here and there. But she was a long way from a hundred pieces. She settled the money belt back in place and went about her business among the grapevines.

Sheba returned to the cabin at dusk with a bucket brimming with shiny blue huckleberries. Joe Nathan strode along beside her, laughing and stealing berries from her bucket.

"Um-umh!" said Joe Nathan, his mouth full of berries. "Next to the master's grapes, these are the best-tasting things on Alston Plantation!"

"Here, Ma," said Sheba. "Take this bucket 'fore Joe Nathan cleans it out."

"You best be sticking to huckleberries," said Marina.

"What you mean, Mama Marina?" asked Joe Nathan.

"I mean forget about the master's grapes. They's conjured."

"Conjured!" cried Joe Nathan. "Who put a spell on them grapes?"

"I did," said Mama Marina.

"Ma!" exclaimed Sheba. "Everybody on Alston Plantation looks forward to ripe grape time. How come you do such a thing?"

Marina patted her belly where the money belt lay hidden. "I done it for a few more miles on your road to freedom."

"Ma, I know how firm your head be set on buying my freedom," said Sheba. "And I know you can do things other folks can't do. But freedom is bought with hard shiny gold."

Joe Nathan turned away from Sheba and her mother.

"Wait!" cried Sheba. "I'll take no freedom without Joe Nathan. We go together, or we stay as slaves."

Mama Marina looked at the two young slaves so much in love with each other.

"Put your trust in me," she said. "Before the grapevines fruit again, you'll both be free."

The word went out that very night. "Mama Marina done put a spell on the grapes!"

No slave would risk popping a single grape into his or her mouth.

The children were warned. "Eat one of them grapes and lizards and snakes will grow inside you. They'll sap your strength and shrivel you up till you're skin and bones and you can't even walk. Before you die, you'll be squirming around on your belly like a serpent and pleading in the unknown tongue."

Mama Marina's name was whispered throughout the plantation the next day.

In the wet rice paddies they asked, "How come she done such a thing?"

Tending the indigo fields they complained, "Never thought I'd see the day when she use her powers against us. Never thought she'd side with the master."

In the stables Joe Nathan overheard the men talking. "Mama Marina done took the sweetness out of fall. Leaves a sour taste in your mouth, don't it?"

The whispering abruptly stopped when Sheba drew near. They might be angry with Mama Marina, but no one wanted to cross her. Crossing a conjure woman could be much worse than missing out on a mess of sugary grapes.

The long steamy summer dragged on into the hot, humid dog days of August. The grapevines thrived in the damp heat. Clusters of fat green grapes swelled to bursting. Never had the vines borne such a weight of fine fruit. But dog days were trying times for humans. Tempers were short. Dogs ran mad. Rattlesnakes struck without warning. Sores wouldn't heal, and mildew covered everything. Master Alston seemed more out of sorts than usual.

One sultry day he sent for Joe Nathan.

"I been thinking, Joe boy," he said. "You got so good at leather working I could make a fair amount on you. You turn out the finest harnesses, shoes, and belts in the county."

"Thank you, sir," replied Joe Nathan. He wondered what the master was leading up to.

"I'm thinking come winter, when the work's slack around here, I could rent you out to other plantations that need harnesses and shoes for their slaves."

"But sir, they's plenty of work here in winter," said Joe Nathan.

"Well, you can train one of the boys to keep things in shape here," said Master Alston. "I'll do better keeping you on the road all year round, good as you are at leather working. My mind's made up."

Joe Nathan was dripping with sweat, but he felt as cold as the heart of winter. Staying on the road all year round meant being driven by one harsh slave master after another. That he might be able to endure. But never seeing Sheba was more than he could bear.

"Get on back to your work, boy. Next trip to Charleston, I'm buying you a traveling suit. You got to look decent if I'm to get the price I'll be asking for you."

Sheba wept. At first she cried out and pounded the floor with her fists. Mama Marina held her tight, rocked her, and sang to her in a strange language that Sheba didn't understand. Finally her cries eased off, but tears slid from her eyes for days after.

Joe Nathan cut and hammered and sewed his leather like one possessed. He stopped speaking. Every night he sat holding Sheba's hand while her silent tears glistened in the moonlight.

Mama Marina walked alone at midnight up and down the rows of conjured grapes. She called on the spirits to show her a way.

On the third night she walked the vineyards in total darkness. As the rumble of distant thunder sounded, she raised her arms and summoned the spirits. An earthshaking thunderclap crashed around her, and for a blinding moment lightning slashed through the vineyard, turning the vines to silver.

It was over in an instant. Again Mama Marina was enveloped in darkness. But inside her head a shining light blazed, showing her the way she had been seeking.

The next night Mama Marina led Sheba and Joe Nathan into the conjured vineyard. She pulled two bunches of grapes from a vine and gave one to Joe Nathan, the other to Sheba.

"Eat!" she commanded.

They both held the grapes without moving. What could she mean? The grapes were conjured. They'd surely die if they ate them.

"Eat, I tell you," snapped Mama Marina. "You'll go down through the valley of the shadow of death. But you won't die. You'll come out of that valley two free souls."

Sheba began to tremble. She uttered a small desperate cry and stifled the sound by pushing the grapes into her mouth.

Joe Nathan slowly and silently raised the grapes to his mouth.

The two of them swallowed the sharp, green, unripe grapes.

From that night Sheba's tears stopped flowing. Joe Nathan talked again, and even sang as he worked the leather.

The weather turned cool, and the green grapes put on a blush of color as they began to sweeten. Master Alston was pleased to see such a fine crop. He was mighty pleased to have figured a way to keep the slaves from robbing his vines. "They fall for that mumbo-jumbo stuff every time!" he said, and laughed.

The slaves harvested all the grapes. And not a single grape did any slave taste. Master Alston laughed again when he saw the slaves washing their hands after handling the grapes.

After the harvest, Master Alston made his trip to Charleston and brought back a traveling suit for Joe Nathan.

"Soon, by Christmas at the latest," said the master, "I'll be renting Joe Nathan out for good money."

The fear of separation seized Sheba and Joe Nathan again. A few nights later there was an early frost. The leaves on the grapevines shriveled and turned brown. That same night Sheba tossed and turned and was plagued with bad dreams. When morning came, she could hardly drag herself out of bed. Her joints ached, her head was hot, and she felt dizzy when she stood up.

When Joe Nathan failed to turn up at the stables, they found him in his bed burning up with fever and talking out of his head.

Mama Marina brewed a strong tea of St. John's weed and rabbit tobacco and dosed them both. Their fevers cooled, but they remained weak. They couldn't eat. And their young faces looked sad and drawn.

By Christmastime the grapevines were bare dark branches, lifeless, gnarled and twisted. Sheba had streaks of gray in her hair. She walked bent over like an old woman. Joe Nathan was as thin as a reed. His face was as wrinkled as an old man's, and his fingers were as gnarled as the grapevines. He could no longer work the leather.

Master Alston paid little attention to Sheba, but Joe Nathan was a worry. He'd been rented out to a plantation on the Ashley River, west of Charleston. Now he was too sickly to go. The master brought in a white doctor to examine him.

"Strangest thing I've ever seen," said the doctor. "I can't find any medical reason for this slave's decline."

"Give him a tonic to bring him around!" roared Master Alston.

"He's beyond any tonic I have," said the doctor.

By the middle of winter it appeared that both Sheba and Joe Nathan would surely die.

"Mama," cried Sheba, "I want to believe you. I truly do, but I think I'm dying."

"Hush, child. Hush and sleep. You're passing through the worst of the valley. But you will make it through."

"And Joe Nathan?" Sheba asked weakly.

"Him, too," answered Mama Marina.

One cold day in February, Mama Marina went to see Master Alston.

"Pardon, sir," she said, "but I am sorely troubled. My daughter and Joe Nathan lie dying."

"Two healthy slaves lost in one winter. You know how much that costs me?"

"I know, sir," answered Marina. "Could I ask a question, sir?"

"Go on," said the master.

"How much these two dying slaves be worth?"

"Worth!" boomed the master. "They're worth nothing. Who would buy dying slaves?"

Mama Marina hesitated a moment. Then she said very quietly, "I would, sir."

"I'm not in the mood for jokes, Marina," snapped the master.

"I wasn't joking, sir," she replied. "I'd like to buy freedom for them poor souls. I've put aside all the money I've ever made from my gift of conjuring. It won't buy a well slave, sir. But would you consider taking twenty gold pieces for two dying slaves?"

At first the master was too astonished to speak. Then he took the gold pieces Marina offered.

"You're a fool, Marina," he said as he counted the money.

"Yes, sir," answered Marina.

"No one can say I cheated you. You know what you're getting. You've struck your own bargain. I'll accept it."

"I'll need papers of freedom, sir," said Marina.

It was done. Mama Marina returned with her precious papers to tend Sheba and Joe Nathan. Neither of them could rise from their beds. They lay shivering under piles of quilts, looking older than the oldest slaves on the plantation. It was whispered in the slave quarters that Sheba and Joe Nathan had eaten the conjured grapes.

Mama Marina made no effort to quiet the rumors. Instead, she sought out old Johnnycake. He made the monthly trip to Charleston to pick up supplies for Master Alston.

"Johnnycake, I come to collect on a favor," said Mama Marina.

"Name it," said old Johnnycake. "I stood in your debt more than once over the years."

"I need you to take something to Charleston for me."

"Name it," repeated Johnnycake.

"Lean your ear close," said Mama Marina. "I don't want even the wind to hear what I tell you."

It was early March before old Johnnycake set the day for the Charleston trip. Tiny bumps were on the bare, black, twisted grapevines. With a few sunny days they would burst into buds. Sheba and Joe Nathan, who had been more dead than alive, began to stir. When Mama Marina brought them cornmeal gruel, they gulped it down like starved dogs.

A week later, in the early dawn before daylight, old Johnnycake drove his wagon to Mama Marina's cabin. Now Sheba and Joe Nathan were able to walk on their own, and with a little help they climbed into the wagon.

"Hold on to the freedom papers," said Mama Marina, "and go straight to the Quaker meeting house when you reach Charleston."

The two young people hugged Mama Marina and crawled under a quilt in the back of the wagon.

Mama Marina followed the wagon as far as the vineyard. There she stopped and watched until it turned onto the Charleston road and disappeared.

She walked through the vineyard, examining the vines. Tiny leaves were popping out. Soon the vines would be fully leafed, and clusters of grapes would follow. As the grapes ripened, Sheba and Joe Nathan would come again into the full bloom of their youth.

"That's when I'll take the spell off the grapes," said Mama Marina. "That's when my children will be free."